Tom and Ricky
and the
Haunted House Mystery

Bob Wright

High Noon Books
Novat

Cover Design: Nancy Peach
Interior Illustrations: Herb Heidinger

Glossary: print, press, fake, mansion, fence, dent, battery, flashlight

International Standard Book Number: 0-87879-399-2

10 09 08 07 06 05 04
15 14 13 12 11 10 09 08

Contents

CHAPTER 1

Thump. Bang. Thump. Bang.

Ricky stopped his bike. He was on Front Street. He was waiting for Tom. They were going to meet at West's Video Store.

"Ricky! Ricky!" Someone was calling. Maybe it was Tom. It wasn't. It was Eddie.

"Eddie, where are you going?" Ricky asked.

"I'm on my way to Miles Print Shop," Eddie answered.

"Miles Print Shop? What's up?" Ricky asked.

"I have to pick up some things there for my mother. What are you doing?" Eddie asked.

"I'm waiting for Tom. But he's late again. We were going to look at some of the new video games," Ricky said.

"Come on with me. It won't take long. The print shop is near here. We'll be right back," Eddie said.

"OK. If it won't take too long," Ricky said.

"It's just down the street," Eddie said.

Ricky got back on his bike. They parked their bikes in front of the print shop.

Thump. Bang. Thump. Bang. Thump. Bang. Mr. Miles had a lot of work going on. His printing press was making a lot of noise.

Mr. Miles saw the boys. "Come on in," he said.

"I'm here to get some things you printed. They are for my mother," Eddie said.

"That's right. And here they are. They're all ready for you," Mr. Miles said.

"What's all that?" Ricky asked.

"It's for the P.T.A.," Eddie answered.

"That's a lot of paper. Here. Let me wrap it up for you. You can carry it better on your bike," Mr. Miles said.

Thump. Bang. Thump. Bang.

"What did you say?" Eddie asked.

"I said I'll wrap it up for you," Mr. Miles yelled.

3

"My mother will be in today to pay you,"

Eddie said.

"That will be fine," Mr. Miles said.

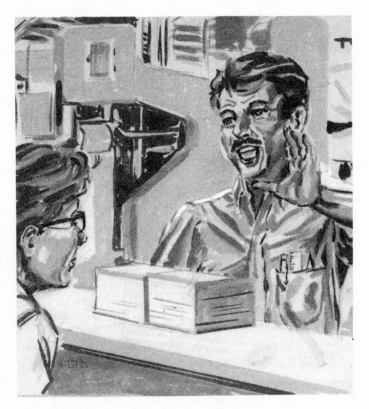

"I said I'll wrap it up for you,"
Mr. Miles yelled.

The boys walked back to their bikes.

"Boy, it was hard to hear anything in there," Ricky said.

"It sure was. Come on. Let's go back to the video store," Eddie said. They got back on their bikes.

By this time Tom was at the video store. Ricky could see him waiting in front.

"Where have you been? I've been waiting here a long time," Tom said.

"A long time? We just left to go to the print shop," Ricky said.

"OK. OK. I was just kidding," Tom said.

"Come on. Let's go into the store," Ricky said.

5

Just then Mr. West came out. "I'm sorry, boys. I have to close the store. It will open later," he said.

Then Sergeant Collins walked out of the store.

"What's up, Sergeant Collins?" Ricky asked their friend.

Mr. West has to count his money," the Sergeant said.

"Did someone rob him?" Tom asked.

"You might say someone did," the Sergeant answered.

"How's that?" Ricky asked.

"Someone gave him some funny money," the Sergeant answered.

CHAPTER 2

Funny Money

Funny money? The boys looked at Sergeant Collins. They didn't know what he meant.

"What's funny money?" Eddie asked.

"Do you mean play money like money from a game?" Tom asked.

"No. Play money doesn't look real. The money Mr. West has looks real," the Sergeant answered.

"You mean he has fake money?" Ricky asked.

"That's right," the Sergeant said.

"But how does he know it isn't real?" Tom asked.

"There are a lot of ways. When Mr. West called me, he said he was counting his money. He was getting ready to open the store. Then he saw green all over his hands," the Sergeant said.

"You mean the green came off the money?" Ricky asked.

"That's right. If money is real, the green won't come off," the Sergeant said.

"What are you going to do?" Ricky asked.

"I have to find out if there is any more of that funny money in town," the Sergeant said.

"What if there is?" Eddie asked.

"Then we have to find out who is using it.

Someone is breaking the law," the Sergeant said.

"Can we help?" Ricky asked.

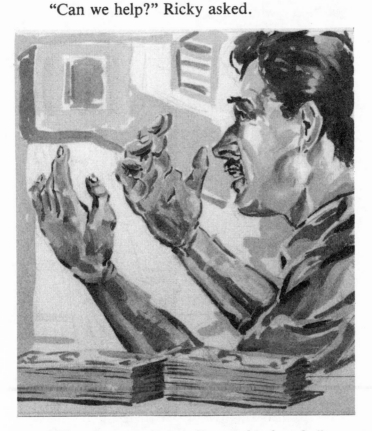

"Then he saw green all over his hands,"
the Sergeant said.

"Not right now. I have some work to do," the Sergeant said. Then he got in his car and left.

"Now what shall we do?" Tom asked.

"Let's ride out to the Pine Mansion," Eddie said.

"The Pine Mansion? Why?" Ricky asked.

"They're going to tear it down," Eddie said.

"Tear it down? Why?" Tom asked.

"No one has lived there for a long time. It's falling down. They're going to put in a park for the kids," Eddie said.

"Come on, Tom. Let's ride out there," Ricky said.

"It's too far away. We'll never get there," Tom said.

"It's not that far away. It's only about a mile. We can go there. When we come back, the video store will be open. Come on," Ricky said.

"OK. Let's go," Tom said.

"Do you think it's really haunted?" Eddie asked.

"The Pine Mansion?" Tom asked.

"That's what I heard. People say they see things moving around in it at night," Eddie said.

"I'm not going," Tom said.

"This is day time, Tom. It will be OK," Eddie said.

"Anyway, we aren't going in it," Ricky said.

"We aren't? Why not? It looks OK to me," Tom said.

"You can't get in it. There's a big fence around it. That's how they keep people out," Ricky said.

"OK. Come on. Let's go," Tom said.

They got on their bikes. They rode down Front Street. Then they turned on to Pine Street. They went down Pine Street a long way. There weren't many houses now. They kept on riding. Then they saw it. It was on a little hill.

"There it is," Ricky called out.

CHAPTER 3

The Pine Mansion

The boys kept on riding their bikes. They wanted to get close to the old Pine Mansion. They stopped by the fence.

"What a big place that is," Ricky said.

"Why is it all falling down? Look. Everything is broken," Tom said.

"It was one of the first houses in town. Mr. and Mrs. Pine were very, very rich. They moved away years ago," Eddie said.

"How do you know all that?" Tom asked.

"I read the story in a book I have," Eddie answered.

"Why did they move away?" Tom asked.

"They owned a lot of land around here. They tried to grow cotton. But it wouldn't grow. So they left and went somewhere else," Eddie said.

"Why do they say it's haunted?" Tom asked.

"After Mr. Pine left, he died. The people who bought it said they saw Mr. Pine. They said he was walking around the house," Eddie said.

"Walking around the house?" Tom asked.

"Not him. Something that looked like him. Those people left. No one ever wanted to live in it after that," Eddie said.

14

"That must have been a long time ago," Ricky said.

"It sure was. It was about fifty years ago," Eddie said.

All of a sudden Ricky said, "Look!"

Tom jumped. "What? What did you see?" he asked.

"The fence is broken over there. Let's go over there," Ricky said.

"Not me," Tom said.

"Oh, come on. We'll just look around," Eddie said.

The boys went over to the broken fence. Ricky stepped over it. "See. I'm OK," he said.

Tom and Eddie walked over to the fence.

"Come on. Let's walk a little closer to the house," Ricky said.

The boys started to walk over to the old Pine Mansion.

"What are you boys doing?" A man called out.

"Did you hear that?" Ricky asked.

A man came walking out of the house.

"We were just looking around," Ricky said.

"Well, you shouldn't be here," the man said.

"What are *you* doing here?" Eddie asked.

"I take care of this place," the man said.

"Do you live here?" Ricky asked.

"No one lives here. I'm just here each day," the man said.

16

"When are they going to tear it down?"
Eddie asked.

"In two weeks," the man said.

"What are you boys doing?"
a man called out.

"Is this place haunted?" Tom asked.

"That's what they say. I wouldn't know. I'm not here at night," the man said.

"Can we look inside?" Eddie asked.

"No, you can't. You boys ask too many questions. Get out of this place," the man said. Then he walked back into the old mansion.

"He was getting mad," Ricky said.

"He could have let us get just one look," Eddie said.

The boys walked back to the fence.

"Look. That old white car must be his," Ricky said.

"His car looks as bad as the house," Tom said.

"What do you mean?" Eddie asked.

"Look at it. Look at all the dents in it," Tom said.

The boys stopped and looked at the car. It was all banged up.

"I don't see how it even runs," Ricky said.

"Get away from that car! Get moving," the man called out.

"Look. He's back on the steps again," Ricky said.

"OK. OK. We're going," Eddie called back.

The man went back inside the house.

"I have an idea," Eddie said.

"What's that?" Ricky asked.

"Let's come back tonight," Eddie said.

"Are you kidding?" Tom asked.

"No. I really mean it. No one will be here. We can see if the house is really haunted," Eddie said.

"Not me," Tom said.

"We won't do anything. We'll just look around," Eddie said.

"Do you think it will be OK?" Tom asked.

"We'll just look at the house. That man won't be here," Ricky answered.

The boys got back to their bikes.

"Come on. Mr. West must have his store open by now," Ricky said.

"Do you think Sergeant Collins found any more funny money?" Tom asked.

"We can ask him when we get back to town," Ricky said.

The boys started back.

It was getting hot by now.

There were no cars on the road. But all of a sudden a car went by them. It was going very fast.

"Did you see that?" Ricky called out.

"I sure did. It was the white car. The one with all the dents," Tom said.

"Didn't that man say he had to stay there all day long?" Eddie asked.

"That's what he said," Ricky answered.

"Then why is he going to town?" Eddie asked.

CHAPTER 4

More Funny Money

The boys were tired when they got to town. It seemed a long way back. It was getting hotter.

"Boy, I'm tired," Tom said.

"We'll cool off," Ricky said.

"Come on. Let's get over to the video store," Eddie said.

Just then Ricky saw Sergeant Collins' police car. "Sergeant Collins!" he called out.

Sergeant Collins heard Ricky. He stopped his car. "What's up?" he asked.

"Have you seen any more funny money?" Ricky asked.

"I sure have. It's all over town. Someone is sure getting it around," Sergeant Collins said.

"How is it getting around so fast?" Ricky asked.

"Someone, or some people, are going around buying things. They pay for things with big bills but they only buy little things. So they get a lot of change," the Sergeant said.

"I don't get it," Tom said.

"A man went into Mr. West's store to buy a 50 cent battery. But the man gave Mr. West a $20 bill. So the man got $19.50 back in real money," the Sergeant said.

"I get it. That's how it works," Tom said.

"Right. So I'm telling everyone to be careful about big bills," the Sergeant said.

"That's a good idea," Eddie said.

"Where have you been? You all look hot and tired," the Sergeant said.

"We rode out to the Pine Mansion. Boy, that man out there isn't very nice," Tom said.

"What man?" the Sergeant asked.

"The man who is taking care of the place," Ricky answered.

"I didn't know there was someone doing that," the Sergeant said.

"We wanted to look around. A man told us to go away," Ricky said.

"That's funny," the Sergeant said.

"What's funny about it?" Ricky asked.

"The town had a man out there at one time. The town let him live there for nothing. All he had to do was to take care of the place. But that man moved away two years ago," the Sergeant said.

"Maybe this new man is just living there. Maybe he wants a free place to live," Eddie said.

"Maybe you're right. But I still have to look into it," the Sergeant said.

Then Tom said, "Come on. Let's see those new video games."

"I have to go. I'll see you boys later," the Sergeant said. He got in his car and left.

25

"What about tonight?" Tom asked.

"What do you mean?" Ricky asked.

"Are we going to ride out to the Pine Mansion?" Tom asked.

"I want to," Eddie said.

"I do, too. Come on, Tom. It won't be hot. It will give us something to do," Ricky said.

"OK. Where shall we meet?" Tom asked.

"Let's all meet at my house at 6:30," Ricky answered.

Then they all went into Mr. West's store.

CHAPTER 5

Funny Lights

That night Tom and Eddie got to Ricky's house.
It was 6:30. Ricky came out to meet them.

"All ready, everyone?" Ricky asked.

"I am," Eddie said.

"Me, too," Tom said.

"I'm glad it's not hot. This will be an easy
ride," Ricky said.

They all got on their bikes. Then they
started for Pine Street. It didn't seem to take long
to get to Pine Mansion.

They got there at 7:00. It was starting to get dark.

"Let's put our bikes here by the fence," Ricky said.

"That's a good idea. Then we can find them in the dark," Eddie said.

"Did anyone bring a flashlight?" Tom asked.

"I did," Ricky said.

"I forgot mine. One is better than none," Eddie said.

"How long are we going to stay here?" Tom asked.

"Not long. We just want to look around," Ricky said.

"I'm glad that man isn't here," Eddie said.

The boys walked up to the front of the house. They looked all around. Then they started up the stairs.

"I thought these stairs would fall down. But they hold us," Tom said.

"Maybe this place isn't as bad as everyone says it is," Ricky said.

There were ten stairs. When they got to the top, Eddie said, "Now how do we get in?"

"Let's see if we can open the door," Ricky said.

Ricky pushed on the door. It opened.

"Look at that. It's so dark in there," Tom said.

The boys looked into the house. They couldn't see anything.

"Turn on your flashlight, Ricky," Tom said.

Ricky shined his flashlight into the house. Everything looked old and broken. Ricky walked in. "Come on in. It's OK."

Eddie and Tom walked in. They all walked to the end of a big room.

Then Tom stopped. "Did you hear that?" he asked.

"Hear what?" Ricky asked.

"That's just me. I stepped on some paper on the floor," Eddie said. Eddie bent down. He picked up some paper.

"What do you have?" Ricky asked.

"I don't know now. I'll look at it later," Eddie said. He put the paper in his coat.

"I hear something again," Tom said.

Eddie bent down. He picked up some paper.

Eddie and Ricky stopped. They could hear Thump. Bang. Thump. Bang. Thump. Bang.

"What is that?" Ricky asked.

"I don't know. But I don't like it," Tom said.

"Look. I see a light. It's coming from over there," Ricky said.

They all looked at a door. There was light coming from under it.

"I thought no one lived here," Tom said.

"That's what we thought," Ricky said.

The light went out. Then it went on. Then it went off.

"What's going on?" Tom asked.

"Let's get out of here," Eddie said.

"Come on!" Ricky yelled.

They all ran out the front door and down the stairs. Then they ran to their bikes.

"Do you think that place is haunted?" Tom asked.

"I don't know. But all of this sure is funny," Ricky said.

"Did we really see those lights?" Tom asked.

"We sure did," Ricky said.

"And we all heard that thump-bang!" Eddie said.

"I know I've heard that before. But where?" Ricky said.

"Come on. Let's get going," Tom said.

The three boys got on their bikes. They started back for home.

CHAPTER 6

The Next Day

The next day Tom met Ricky at the video store. Then Eddie got there.

"Want to go back to the Pine Mansion?" Eddie asked.

"Not me. No way," Tom said.

"I was just kidding," Eddie said.

"Come on. Let's go in. I want to see what new things Mr. West has," Ricky said.

The three boys walked into the store. They started looking at all the things Mr. West had.

"How are you boys doing today?" Mr. West asked.

"We want to look at the new games," Ricky said.

"I have some good video games. They're used. But they work just fine. They are only $5 each," Mr. West said.

"Where are they?" Eddie asked.

"Right over there," Mr. West said.

"Oh, boy," Eddie said.

They walked over to the used games part of the store. They looked over all the games. Then Eddie said, "Look! Here's The Box Game. It's only been out a week. I'm going to buy it. What a deal this is!"

"Did you find something you want to buy?" Mr. West asked.

"I'm going to buy The Box Game," Eddie said.

"I just got that today. You got a good game. And it's only $5," Mr. West said.

Eddie took five $1 bills out of his coat. "Here you are, Mr. West," Eddie said.

Mr. West took the money. He looked at Eddie's hands. Then he looked at his own hands. They were both green.

"Eddie, what's going on?" Mr. West asked.

"What do you mean?" Eddie asked.

"Look at your hands. Look at mine," Mr. West said.

Mr. West rubbed each $1 bill. The green came off two of them. "Eddie, two of those bills are funny money. I better call Sergeant Collins."

Mr. West rubbed each $1 bill.
The green came off two of them.

"What did I do?" Eddie asked.

"Where did you get that money?" Mr. West asked.

"I don't know," Eddie said.

"I'm not mad, Eddie. We need to know where you got that money," Mr. West said. Then he called Sergeant Collins.

The Sergeant got there right away. He talked to Mr. West and the boys. He looked at the funny money.

"I don't know. My mother gave me $3 for helping her last week," Eddie said.

"What about the other $2?" Ricky asked.

"They were in my coat this morning," Eddie said.

"Wait! I think I know what all of this is about," Ricky yelled.

"Let's hear it, Ricky," Sergeant Collins said.

Ricky started to talk. "We went out to the Pine Mansion last night. We didn't think anyone would be there. We saw lights go on and off. We heard funny things. Eddie stepped on some paper. He picked it up. Then he put it in his coat," Ricky said.

"What are you saying, Ricky?" Tom asked.

"I think the thump—bang we heard was a printing press. One just like the one Mr. Miles has. I think Eddie picked up the funny money at the Pine Mansion. I think those men are printing funny money there at night," he said.

CHAPTER 7

The Mystery is Cleared Up

Sergeant Collins didn't say anything. Everyone just looked at Ricky.

"You could be right, Ricky. No one should be at the Pine Mansion. Maybe people are printing money there," the Sergeant said. He went to the phone. He called the police station.

"What did they say?" Ricky asked.

"I asked them to send two cars out to the Mansion. They'll call us back. We'll just have to wait," the Sergeant said.

It seemed like a long time. Then a call came in for Sergeant Collins. He talked with some other policemen. Then he came over to Tom, Ricky, Eddie, and Mr. West.

"What did they say?" Ricky asked.

"You were right, Ricky. They found the printing press. Three men were printing funny money at night. One man stayed at the Mansion all day. The other two came into town each day. They were buying lots of things. That's how they got rid of the money," the Sergeant said.

"I'm glad you went with me to Mr. Miles' Print Store," Eddie said.

"I'm glad Tom was late so I could go," Ricky said.

"You mean I helped by being late?" Tom asked.

"You sure did," Sergeant Collins said.

"Did they get all the men?" Ricky asked.

"They sure did. They have them at the police station right now. There won't be any more funny money around town," the Sergeant said.

"Then the house wasn't haunted," Tom said.

"No, it wasn't They wanted you to think it was. They wanted you to get out of it," the Sergeant said.

Ricky turned to Eddie. "You don't look very well. What's up?"

"Now I can't get that new game," Eddie said.

"You boys helped get those men. You can have that game. And wait. Here's your $3 back," Mr. West said.

"Thanks, Mr. West," Eddie said.

"There's one thing I don't get about all of this," Tom said.

"What's that?" the Sergeant asked.

"Why did the green come off the funny money?" Tom asked.

"Those men didn't wait for the money to dry. They thought it was dry. But they didn't rub it," the Sergeant said.

Eddie took the $3 out of his coat. "If they had rubbed it, it would have been like this real money."

"Wait! Look! Green is coming off that money," Ricky said.

"You mean this is funny money, too?" Eddie asked.

Ricky looked at Sergeant Collins and Mr. West. They all started to laugh.

"Just kidding, Eddie. Just kidding," Ricky said.